Ice Skater Extraordinaire

Based on the episode written by Krista Tucker
Adapted by Krista Tucker
Illustrated by the Disney Storybook Art Team

HARPER FESTIVAL
An Imprint of HarperCollinsPublishers

ISBN 978-0-06-284395-1

Typography by Brenda E. Angelilli/Scott Petrower
18 19 20 21 22   SCP   10 9 8 7 6 5 4 3 2 1
❖
First Edition

Ooh La La!

I like to imagine I am an ice skater extraordinaire! That's fancy for extraordinary. I do fancy leaps and spins. The crowd adores me! **Ta-da!**

I'm practically an expert at skating in my living room, so I thought I'd be even better on ice. I only tripped and fell once when JoJo threw the flowers before I took my curtsy. A curtsy is a fancy move ice skaters do at the end of their dance.

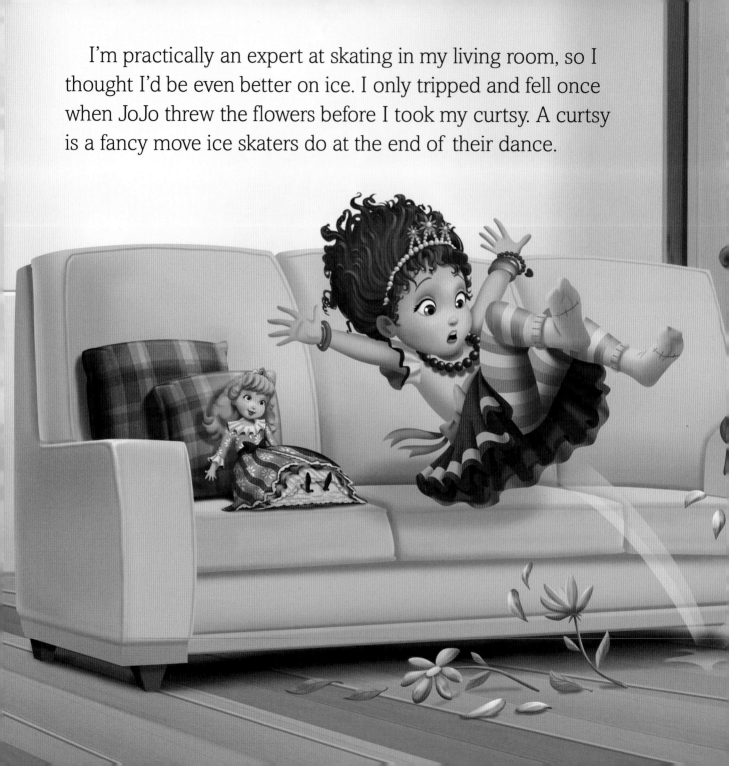

The first time I went to a real ice rink was with my best friend, Bree. I was going to leap and spin and twirl.

I got my rental skates, but they looked tattered.
That's fancy for old.

Bree and I used ribbons and hair clips to fancy them up.

Voilà!

We headed onto the ice. Time to be extraordinary!
But I kept falling down. The ice was slipperier than my
living room. I was lucky Bree was there to help me!

I was almost one hundred percent positive my skates
were broken, but Mom said I just needed to practice.
She brought me a walker to help me stay balanced.

I felt disappointed. I thought I was going to be extraordinary. I told Bree the bad, awful, terrible news. She said she used a walker when she started skating too.

I told Bree if I couldn't be an extraordinary skater, I just wouldn't skate at all! Bree decided to skate without me.

Then I remembered that having fun and skating with Bree was what mattered.

But there was just one thing
we needed to do first.

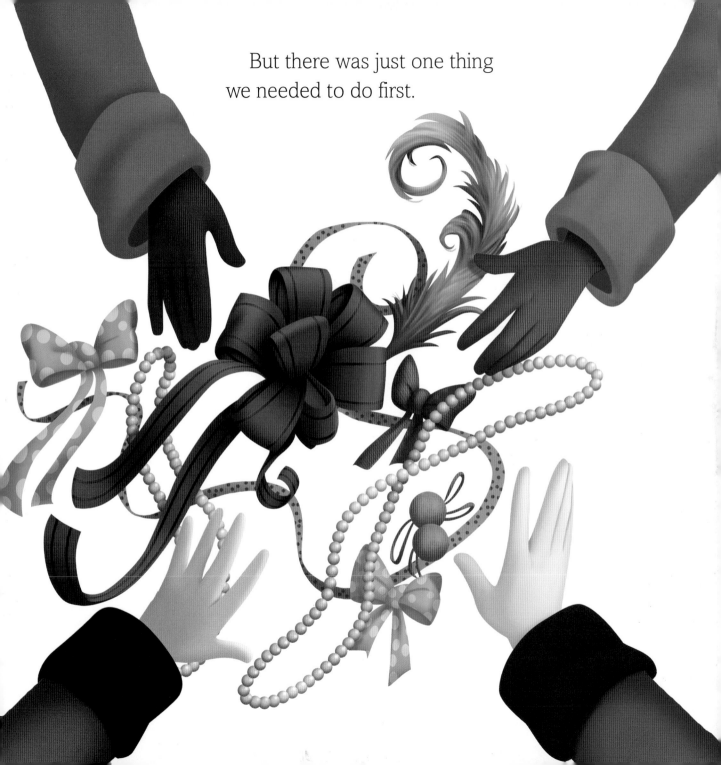

Ooh La La!

Now the walker was
something I could use!

We headed onto the ice. Bree gave me tips. She said to
glide more than step and look where you are going.

I practiced and practiced and soon improved!
Maybe one day I'll be an ice skater extraordinaire.
But for now, it's extraordinary to go ice skating with
my best friend.

Checklist for your Fancy day at the ice rink

- ☐ Ice skates (psst! Adding ribbons, pom-poms, and bows will make your skates look extra fancy!)

- ☐ A walker if your balance is wobbly

- ☐ Warm mittens or gloves

- ☐ A glittery scarf

- ☐ Cozy earmuffs or a hat

- ☐ A friend to help you up when you fall down

- ☐ Lots of patience if you're still learning

- ☐ A sparkly attitude